Pablo Helguera

THE WITCHES OF TEPOZTLÁN

(AND OTHER UNPUBLISHED OPERAS)

THE WITCHES OF TEPOZTLÁN

(AND OTHER UNPUBLISHED OPERAS)

A Critical Study

by

Pablo Helguera

Translated from the Spanish by Noël Baca Castex

Jorge Pinto Books Inc.
New York

So my voice at the center of the four
fundamental voices
would have on its shoulders
the weight of the birds of paradise.

Carlos Pellicer

The first one remembers what the second
one understands and the third one wishes;
the second one
understands what the first one remembers
and the third one wishes;
the third one wishes what the first one
remembers and the second one
understands.

R. Lull, *Libri Contemplationis in Deum*, 1274

To Elsa Lizalde,
for whom opera was always paradise.

(1942–2006)

Contents

PREFACE TO THE ENGLISH EDITION

I am amongst those who believe that in art, like in eroticism, the potential of seduction, if any, is greatly based on the simple principle of concealment. This is why I often refrain from making any public explanatory remarks about projects like this one. But in the case of this work, given its removal from its original language and context, I thought I should provide a brief background.

The idea for this book was born in Mexico City in 2007, during the planning stages of an exhibition at the Enrique Guerrero Gallery. The exhibition consisted of a historical display of stage-set dioramas, set-design sketches, musical excerpts, and a full video documentary summarizing the plots, biographies and interpretative views of the operas whose stories are contained in this volume.

My incursion into the realm of biographical exhibitions in contemporary art spaces started in 1998, in Mexico City as well. At a small artist-run space called Tallería, I presented an exhibit entitled *Estacionamientos* (Parking Zones), which displayed the works of fourteen artists of different ages, backgrounds, nationalities, esthetic inclinations, and artistic skills. These artists ranged from a religious 23 year-old Argentinean man; to a 40-something, London-based, Egyptian female artist who made installations on airplane crashes with hanging pillows and sand; to a 50 year-old Polish minimalist artist influenced by Dan Flavin; and so forth. My work was also included in that show. On opening day, the question of whether these artists were fictional or not did not come up; another question that did not come up was whether the biographies, artist statements, published criticisms, and published retorts to those criticisms had been written by a single person. In the end, the works were real and that seemed to suffice. What the project did incite, however, is the question of the relationship between biography and artistic voice: How influential, or relevant, is it for a viewer to know that the work he or she is looking at has been made by, say, an unknown 90 year-old Japanese artist living in a remote village, or by a rising young artist living in New York City today?

My interest in biography as the intersection of scholarship and literature was fueled by my reading, as a student, of classic biographical literature such as Plutarch's *Parallel Lives*, Boswell's *Life of Johnson* and, particularly, two works of contrasting periods and approaches: Marcel Schwob's *Imaginary Lives* (1896), a symbolist work that was popularized in Latin America by Jorge Luis Borges; and John Aubrey's *Brief Lives*, a foundational book on the modern art of biography written at the end of the seventeenth century.

I was, and still am, intrigued by two things: the way in which a biography almost inevitably becomes a powerful context for the interpretation of an artist's work, and the way in which the ruthlessness of historical perspective ends up shaping the final collective judgment of artists (whether the artist in question has intended it this way or not). This curiosity has led me to other unusual life stories that I eventually turned into other exhibitions of their own, such as that of Florence Foster Jenkins, the infamous diva who is considered the worst soprano in history and yet was greatly admired for her determination, innate showmanship, and incomparable flair; Friedrick Froebel, the inventor of Kindergarden, who died believing that he had failed to create a successful educational system; and Giulio Camillo, a Renaissance mystic who tried to envision a "memory theater"—a place where all the things of the world could be known. This last project, entitled *Parallel Lives*, was presented as a performance at New York's Museum of Modern Art in 2003. The exhibition was based less on the frontier between fiction and history and more on the alchemy-like potential of comparative biography, while also making visual and thematic relationships, almost in the manner of a Baroque fugue.

It was projects like these, along with my continued interest in the ideas of biographical fiction, thematic counterpoint, and the blurring line between the artist's work and his or her life, that led to the idea for *Las brujas de Tepoztlán*. Furthermore, the fact that this project deals with classical music presents an additional dimension that is largely absent in contemporary art, namely the marked differentiation between composer and interpreter—something that, when transposed to the realm of the visual arts, provides an interesting perspective on authorship.

The original goal of this book was to function as an exhibition guide—or, perhaps, a "playbill" with program notes—so it was envisioned as a brief tome and not an exhaustive study of art (something akin to what one would read during an intermission). But, like Aubrey's *Brief Lives*, which he originally wrote as reference footnotes for a friend who was working on another book that has now been forgotten, this book is now being sent out on a journey its own, separate from its exhibition, to humbly experience its own biographical fate.

Cobble Hill, Brooklyn, June 2008

PRELUDE

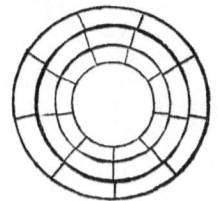

The purpose of this analysis and comparative study is to rescue and share with the public the main aspects of four operas that have remained in obscurity until now, as have their authors: Anselmo Jiménez de la Rueda, Mona Kassem, Richard Pryce, and Enrico Camorelli.

In general, the history of music and art is full of unfinished chapters that describe the accomplishments of only some individuals, while usually skipping certain achievements that perhaps were not understood at the time and eventually fell into oblivion. That is the case of the works discussed in this book, and of its creators, who developed highly innovative musical, dramatic, and esthetic ideas in the times the works were created but, for different reasons, have gone unnoticed until now.

We have decided to do a comparative analysis of these works because, despite the different periods in which they were composed, the four operas reveal a similar spirit and illustrate, each one in its own way and in a complementary manner, crucial aspects of the relationship between the artist and his work, the way it is interpreted, and the role played by history when rewriting these interpretations.

This study, however, which in musical terms should actually be referred to as "divertimento," humbly seeks to go beyond the mere interpretation and rediscovery of these works by analyzing other issues related to historical interpretation and critical commentary, for instance: To what extent does the creative interpretation of the critic or researcher interfere with the work itself, even to the point of replacing it? To what extent are we getting to know a piece through the voice of the person who "discovered" it, or the person who serves as mediator between the time of the composer and today? How does the work change when presented in new contexts, and whom should we give credit to when re-appreciating a work in a new era? It is also worth mentioning that, in the case of historical works such as these, when we receive a message, it is formed by a series of interpretative layers that are difficult to decipher: the composer is speaking through his characters, the singers are giving a voice to the characters, and, finally, the critics and historians are rationalizing the interpretation of the message. In that respect, each work is a multitude of works, with voices that describe it in different moments and periods. So, is there an essential and unique work, or only a variety of equally valid interpretations? And, in the cases in which the critic's interpretation improves the work or the musician elevates the original composition to a more attractive level, is it worth trying to preserve the authenticity of the original piece? None of these questions are completely answered in this project—we can only envision shadows of ideas, as Giordano Bruno wrote.

William Kentridge, an artist, once said that when we watch a theater of shadows and laugh as the shape of a hand forms the shadow of a dog, we are laughing about three things at once: we can see the caricature of the dog itself; we know that a human hand is forming that image; and, finally, we realize we have fallen prey to our own credulity. I would add that it is through this exercise that we can intuitively comprehend that what we see is never complete, or entirely real, or authentic, or altogether explainable. What we see is merely a domesticated image through games and simplified representations of our reality.

It could be said that *The Witches of Tepoztlán* (*and Other Unpublished Operas*) is a sort of theater of shadows in which we have given free reign to the interpretations and parallelisms that the distance of history and the mysteries of oblivion have allowed us to make. We modestly hope that our creative "insolence" is not just that; that the images we have tried to conjure up generate something that goes beyond the distraction of a brief puppet show, and that some of these artists' shadows of ideas are projected beyond the pages of this book.

Pablo Helguera

CHORAL

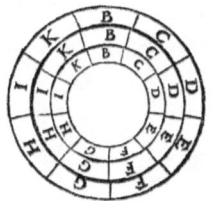

THE WITCHES OF TEPOZTLÁN

(1654)

Anselmo Jiménez de la Rueda

One summer night in 1977, in the sacristy of the church of La Soledad in Seville, Father Carlos Vega accidentally removed a board that served as the bottom surface of an armoire. Underneath the board he found three thick books with a series of birth certificates along with other old documents. Among these documents was a 17th-century manuscript, handwritten by a Mexican composer who, up to that moment, had been practically forgotten.

Before the recent discovery of *Las brujas de Tepoztlán* (The Witches of Tepoztlán), it was considered that the history of opera in the New Spain did not begin until 1708, with the creation of *El Rodrigo* by Manuel de Sumaya. However, *Las brujas de Tepoztlán* by Anselmo Jiménez de la Rueda precedes *El Rodrigo* by more than half a century. This discovery has allowed the opportunity to rectify history and recognize the enormous contribution of this playwright and composer from the Americas.

About the Author

Anselmo Jiménez de la Rueda was born in 1593 in Morelia, Michoacán, and died in 1674 in Mexico City. Little is known about his parents, but certain information indicates that his father, Guillermo Jiménez de

9

la Herrera, was a magistrate and his mother, who was ambiguously described in her marriage certificate as a "foreigner from the mountainous region of Spain," might have been a gipsy. It is known that Jiménez studied music in Morelia under the guidance of Cristóbal de la Encina, the choir director of the town's cathedral at the time. Encina must have noticed Jiménez de la Rueda's talent very early on and requested that Jiménez be offered, at a very young age, the position of choir conductor at the church of Pátzcuaro. An early motet by Jiménez, titled *Salve Regina Eterna* (which would later be incorporated into *Las brujas*) has survived this period. Despite the young musician's precocious talent, however, his father was against his musical calling and, a year later, he arranged for Jiménez to move to Mexico City, where they had relatives, and study law at the University of Mexico City. What we have learned about this period comes from Jiménez's work, in particular his play *La ermita de San Sebastian* (The Hermit of Saint Sebastian), in which he alludes to his years as a student without much enthusiasm. It seems that Jimenez neglected his legal studies and, instead, became an avid reader of treatises and texts on the occult. At university, he's supposed to have discovered the books written by the Jesuit Athanasius Kircher, an increasingly influential writer of that period who was very popular among the intellectuals of the New Spain, beginning with the Mexican nun and poet Sor Juana Inés de la Cruz. In fact, the text of *La ermita* is full of seemingly hidden Kercherian references. These references, however, reveal more of a teenage fascination with intellectual prose than a real understanding of its meaning and, possibly, a desire to penetrate the local intellectual circles by using the conceptual codes that were in vogue at the time. The disdain with which Jiménez refers to his profession in this play also suggests that Jiménez never thrived as a magistrate, perhaps for lack of a real calling or for lack of interest; and that, throughout his life, he had a difficult time trying to reconcile his love of art and his survival through the legal profession.

It was at this university that Jiménez first met Juan Ruiz de Alarcón, who would later be known as the most important playwright of Mexico's colonial era. We know about their friendship, which would eventually turn into rivalry, from Ruiz de Alarcón's own hand. In fact, the two adversaries found in Alarcón's works *El semejante a sí mismo* (The Man Who Resembled Himself) and *El condenado por desconfiado* (The Doubter Damned) are considered to be based directly on Jiménez. It is not clear why Alarcón felt apprehension toward Jiménez. Particularly in Mexico, Alarcón had a unique position in the cultural elite of that time and Jiménez was such an introvert that he was never able to achieve a fraction of the recognition Alarcón would receive.

The art world in Mexico during that period was quite limited and artists fought tooth and nail to displace any rivals. Jiménez, who we know was an extremely feeble and timid character, as well as one of questionable lineage, probably found it difficult to navigate that social circle and most likely could not stand up to Ruiz Alarcón's crushing personality.

In 1615, Jiménez traveled to Spain to work in the Council of the Indies, but his trip was not very successful and, by 1617, he was back in Mexico, penniless and apparently involved in a love affair that would end in a violent scuffle with a Spaniard. Jiménez nearly died in that fight and lost one ear as a result of a wound. After this unfortunate incident, the cruel society of musicians of the New Spain, who disapproved of Jiménez's artistic creation, nicknamed him "el tuerto acústico" (the one-eyed deaf). It is said that Jiménez kept his ear and that it was later stolen by his rivals and occasionally displayed at parties and other celebrations to humiliate the composer.

The few documents that shed light on Jiménez's life include a transfer deed for lands that belonged to his family near Cacahuamilpa, Guerrero; a marriage certificate; and a few letters from Jiménez himself. It is known that, by 1640, Jiménez had opened in the town of Paracho, Michoacán, a luthiery shop that produced viols (this probably began the tradition of producing instruments in that town, which is now famous for that reason). His instruments must have been satisfactory enough for, in 1647, Jiménez was able to persuade the viceregal court to help him finance a trip to Venice in order to buy certain varnishes for his instruments.

It was in Venice that Jiménez saw the first performance of *L'incoronazione di Poppea* (The Coronation of Poppea) by Monteverdi, which is considered one of the first operas in history. The combination of scenery, music and drama had an enormously profound effect on Jiménez, and we could say that it was a life-changing experience, as he later wrote in a letter to his sister:

> ... *before that majestic scene, I heard the most extraordinary melodies, interlacing with one another, and creating a mixed tapestry of incredible voices. It was as if a cathedral of sounds was being built before my eyes.*

Upon his return to Mexico, Jiménez de la Rueda seemed determined to produce comedies that would incorporate the musical elements he had discovered in Italy. He soon became involved with a theater company that put on two of his comedies: *El ogro de la montaña* (The Ogre of the Mountain) and *Las artimañas son encantos* (Artifices are Enchantments), which are now lost.

When his father died, Jiménez sold the land he inherited and devoted himself to writing a piece that, in his view, incorporated the aspects of comedy and music that had originally inspired him in Italy. The result of this was *Las brujas de Tepoztlán*, an opera that is structured as a comedy with musical interludes and a tragic denouement that breaks with the usual form of the genre.

The Italian format and theme of this piece were completely unheard of in the New Spain, something that would later cause difficulties for Jiménez. In a letter, his contemporary, the scientist and philosopher Carlos de Sigüenza y Góngora wrote:

> ... *it is rumored that there is a man from Morelia who is preparing to present a theatrical composition unlike anything seen so far, and that said composition, with poetic turns* à la *Lope de Vega and musical arias, contains numerous references to the indigenous history of the New Spain.*

It was challenging for Jiménez to produce his new composition, however, and it appears that at some point he decided to cancel it. But in 1660, six years after writing the opera, the Cabildo (the municipality of the city) circulated a printed notice announcing seven contests to be celebrated on All Saints Day (November 10). Excited about the contests, Jiménez summoned the help of students of music and theater from the San Pedro y San Pablo School to put on his production.

The preparations took months and it is believed that Jiménez got deep in debt after building an excessively ornate stage with all kinds of symbols that certainly impressed everyone who saw it. A news clipping from that time describes the stage of *Las brujas:*

> *. . . it was decorated with all kinds of tapestries of gold and silk, with several elaborate contraptions and costumes, many flowers, vegetables and trees, fine fabrics and colors, with trumpets and flageolets.*

The presentation of *Las brujas*, however, was a colossal failure. The contest judges were deeply offended by the theme and the strange musical combinations Jiménez had created—which included two or three instruments designed by himself, one of which he called a "polyphonic viol." The same article continues to describe the event:

> *. . . quite big was the audience's surprise when they heard such blasphemies and talk, which seemed to derive from witchcraft, as well as certain demonic sounds that sounded more like bats in a cave than melodies. This caused the author to be booed at and bombarded with shoes and eggplants and any kind of projectiles the spectators had at hand.*

In the early Baroque operas that inspired Jiménez de la Rueda, comedy blended with tragic elements—a highly unusual thing for the times, and particularly unheard of in the New Spain, so it is not surprising that Jiménez's work may have offended the educated sensibilities. It is also said that, in a seemingly envious act, and perhaps sensing an opportunity to hurt his rival, Ruiz de Alarcón helped spread the opinion that the opera's theme was immoral and that "none of that could be seen in Madrid."

The audience's fierce rejection of the work must have been devastating for Jiménez. But, as if the public outcry and the humiliation hadn't been enough, the situation became even worse. The opera was reported to the Inquisition as a blasphemous act and Jiménez narrowly escaped a sentence after renouncing his creation in writing and accepting to destroy the manuscript of the work immediately.

Jiménez spent his last years being the laughingstock of his fellow artists and harassed by the Inquisition, even after destroying the manuscript and sheet music for *Las brujas*. He never wrote music again and, probably distraught by the rejection of what he considered his masterpiece, Jiménez retired from public life. He died soon after, in 1674, run over by a carriage on Donceles Street in Mexico City.

We would not know about this opera today had it not been for a twist of fate: sometime before the premiere of the opera, a copy of the manuscript wound up on the desk of Enrique Gutiérrez de Luna, a printer in Seville, and was never destroyed. This copy got buried amongst other documents in the files found in the church of La Soledad. Evidently, Jiménez had sent a copy of the opera to Spain in the hope that it would be published (very little was published in the Americas at the time and most of those books were of religious nature). But due to neglect, or will, from his part, the composer never mentioned its existence. However, even though the manuscript was found in 1977, its authenticity was not verified until 2005, when, at the Palafoxiana Library in Puebla, a researcher named Ignacio Flores Cano discovered a letter dated in 1655, which Gutiérrez de Luna had sent to Jiménez de la Rueda. In this letter, Gutiérrez de Luna acknowledged receipt of the copy of

Las brujas and informed Jiménez that he would not be able to publish it because, as he tried to put in tactful terms, "he was not sure of who would be interested in such a complex creation."

Synopsis of the Opera

Rinaldo, the main character, is a religious painter who is deeply in love with Dorotea, the daughter of Don Álvaro, the town's sheriff (*El comendador*). Don Álvaro is against Rinaldo's courtship and wants his daughter to marry Torrijos, Rinaldo's old artistic rival. Dorotea, who loves both men, doesn't know whom to choose but, pressured by her father, accepts Torrijos' marriage proposal. This is terrible news for Rinaldo, who contemplates suicide. A friend dissuades him from taking this action and tells him about a witch who lives in a cave in Tepoztlán, who may be able to help ease his pain. Desperate and hoping to forget his past, Rinaldo decides to visit the witch and presents his problem to her. The witch agrees to help Rinaldo but warns him that the forces of evil can be unwieldy and that the effect of her potion might be too powerful. But Rinaldo is determined and willing to try anything at this point and he eagerly drinks the potion that is supposed to fulfill his wish. When he does so, Rinaldo's mind undergoes a prodigious transformation, though not in the way he expected it—it has the opposite effect. Instead of forgetting his past, Rinaldo develops the ability to see the future.

Once back in his workshop, Rinaldo is haunted by powerful images and feels compelled to start painting his increasingly clear visions of the future, as if these were being dictated to him by a divine voice. Rinaldo sees Mexico City in the nineteenth and twentieth centuries. (The way Jiménez de la Rueda imagines the

Mexico of the future is very interesting: a city full of enormous, superimposed pyramids in a kind of Aztec-style Renaissance. This passage in particular, as well as the references to witchcraft and its Hermetic character, were especially condemned by the Inquisition.)

As Rinaldo goes through the process of envisioning the things to come, he is soon able to predict his own future, including his own funeral. But seeing his own funeral does not horrify him as much as the vision that follows, that of Dorothea marrying his enemy, Torrijos. At this point, Rinaldo decides to try to change the course of events instead of accepting the future's inevitability.

With the help of his manservant, Rinaldo devices a secret plan to kill Torrijos so he can marry Dorotea. One night, Rinaldo furtively enters Torrijos' studio and waits for his arrival behind the curtains. But it is Don Álvaro who enters the room in order to grant his daughter's hand to Torrijos. Rinaldo mistakes Don Álvaro for Torrijos and stabs his beloved Dorotea's father. Don Álvaro falls dead as Dorotea and Torrijos enter the scene. Then, in order to avenge Don Álvaro, Torrijos stabs Rinaldo. Dorotea screams in horror when she sees Rinaldo wounded and runs to him, realizing at this point that it is Rinaldo whom she truly loves. But it is too late, for Rinaldo is dying. At that moment, Rinaldo has one last vision: his paintings have transcended history and are admired by future generations. Envisioning his artistic immortality, and knowing that he will be the eternal recipient of Dorotea's love, Rinaldo dies peacefully.

Critical Analysis of the Opera

Las brujas de Tepoztlán was created during the height of the New Spain's seventeenth century and, therefore, includes several aspects of the emerging Gongorism that

Spanish literature was experiencing at that time. The influence of Calderón de la Barca is very clear in the narrative (the idea of a man whose visions separate him from reality, as in *La vida es un sueño [Life Is a Dream]*). Also evident in *Las brujas* is the moralistic aspect of Alarcón's work (illustrated by the protagonist's eventual triumph, if not in love, in artistic posterity). The work's dramatic narrative is consistently dynamic and Jiménez breaks it in half by dedicating a whole act to Rinaldo's visions. In some respects, this act becomes a sort of long interlude that diverges considerably from the opera's main storyline and can be a bit tedious. Nevertheless, aside from its original format, not found in any of the music or theater of the New Spain, or even Spain itself, this opera has some extraordinary aspects. This was the first composition in the New World to experiment with the aspects of the early Baroque opera Jiménez saw in Venice, as well as the first composition that could be called an opera. On the other hand, its contemporary vernacular theme, and the character of the witch in particular, has no precedents (it is thought that Jiménez's witch character was adopted by the Spanish playwright Aníbal Urrieta, who wrote a play titled *La bruja de la morería*, which in turn would be a model for librettist Arrigo Boito for the character of Ulrica, the fortuneteller, in *Un ballo in maschera* by Verdi). Witches or sorceresses were known to exist in colonial times, but few people ever mentioned them. While the famous Salem witch trials date back to 1691, there is substantial recorded evidence of witchcraft cases in New England long before that. Witchcraft was punishable by death in Connecticut as early as 1642. According to historian Matthew Grant, Alse Young of the town of Windsor, was arguably the first woman to be executed for witchcraft in America. She was hanged on

May 26, 1647, at the meeting house square of Hartford, Connecticut. Curiously, a news clipping from 1649 tells about a group of English-speaking witches who had ended up in Tepoztlán, apparently escaping their persecution in New England, and had taken refuge in a cave near the Tepozteco mountain. It is possible that this piece of news, which was well-known when Jiménez wrote *Las brujas*, had an influence in his choice of the theme, even though Tepoztlán was considered a place of magic and supernatural occurrences since pre-Columbian times. (Even today, the city of Tepoztlán is known as an apt place for the practice of alternative medicine and New Age activities.)

In this opera, we can appreciate how Jiménez de la Rueda incorporates a series of Hermetic symbols that reveal a certain defiance against the Christian biblical tradition. Jiménez's intimate knowledge of these symbols, which were difficult to access in the New Spain, has encouraged the speculation that Jiménez's mother had in fact practiced witchcraft. Then again, it is well known that the intellectual personalities of the time and the courtly circles liked to invoke the complex Kabbalistic and Hermetic symbols and emblems (that come from the teachings of Hermes Trismegisto) through the Neo-Platonist filter of the European Baroque. Jiménez skillfully takes advantage of this trend to incorporate symbols that, rather than being Hermetic, belonged to the occult practices associated with magic—which would later alarm the church. However, even the most distrustful critics of Jiménez's work failed to notice the way in which the polyphonic composition of the opera was directly related to the ideas of harmonic creation developed by Robert Fludd in *Ultriusque Cosmi* (1619) and by Kircher in *Misurgia Universalis* (1650). Both Kircher and Fludd, as well as many other Hermeticists, have applied the Pythagorean theories of the harmony of the universe in a way that was literally related to polyphony, as if the universe were an enormous cosmic organ. And Jiménez, at once an Hermeticist and a composer, perhaps thought of himself as the perfect candidate to literalize the mystic harmonies as polyphonic harmonies. This was the first, if not the only, time in the New Spain's history of music that a composer tried to conceptually apply the musical principles described by Fludd as: "Toward the abyss of uncreated matter is the Divine Trinity which, through its divine name, generates three consonant intervals of octaves, fifths and fourths which, according to Pythagorean treatises, produce the complete spectrum of the elemental, celestial and angelical phenomena."[1] The entire musical composition of *Las brujas* is structured in polyphonic intervals of octaves, fifths and fourths—a big departure from the simpler, and more traditional, polyphonic forms of the songs and picaresque ballads that were sung at the time. In terms of sound experimentation, Jiménez was a sort of Varèse of the New Spain.

Which brings us to the heart of the matter: Was *Las brujas* a narrative excuse to conceal a composition with Hermetic codes? I can't answer this question with certainty, for I am not an expert on the obscure Hermetic symbology. But it wouldn't be strange for a creator like Jiménez to have hidden certain messages in a composition with occult and magical concepts to avoid being condemned by the church.

It could be said that, if his aim was to generate a coded message, his attempt failed as his work was condemned by the church anyway. However, even though

---

1   Robert Fludd, *Ultriusque Cosmi*, Vol. 2, Oppenheim, 1916

the Inquisition sensed the implicit heretic nature of the opera, it definitely did not recognize the complexity and sophistication of the various symbols and messages inserted in the work.

At any rate, *Las brujas de Tepoztlán* stands on its own, not because of its unusual theme, but because of its solid narrative and believable characters, as well as its ability to clearly express human emotions and describe perennial themes such as artistic rivalry:

Torrijos
In this surface of colorful delusions,
Little have you achieved
Besides depicting a cataclysm.

Rinaldo
The achievements are there, Torrijos,
But a trained eye is needed,
And yours can see nothing but yourself.

Torrijos
You doubt my eyes,
But no one even looks at you.
You and the art you make
Will fall into oblivion.

Rinaldo
From fearing you, Torrijos, I am far,
Though you think of yourself an authority in
    good taste,
Deaf you are in a city of blind,
Arrogance doesn't paint altarpieces, but mirrors,
And, I must say, you're not an Adonis or an
    ephebe.

Several scholars have noticed that the rivalry between the characters of Torrijos and Rinaldo might illustrate the complex relationship Jiménez and Ruiz de Alarcón had all their life.

Without a doubt, the most interesting and sophisticated passage of *Las brujas* is the moment when Rinaldo sees the future and envisions a great city:

Rinaldo
My eyes give my mind a new view,
As if it and they belonged to someone else,
Seeing this, I can't understand how
This prophecy might be possible.

Hundreds of buildings like mountains,
Pyramidal, infinite, on earth.
Thousands of men inhabit it,
Moving violently to and fro.
Mechanisms of iron and glass
Surround every corner
Like the wind,
Great mobile machines in a race;

Enormous paintings in the sky
With images of shameless women;
I don't see peace at all in the public squares,
But distrust, sadness, and a bloody future;

Is this the city of my tomorrow?
How will we reach this tragic hell?
What sins will we commit, my Lord,
To fall to the bottom of that dark abyss?

Give me refuge, my Lord!
Don't let me witness that present,
Death is better than the iron fences
And the dark gases of that hell on earth!

Though some critics simply allude to the fact that Jiménez had visited several Italian cities, his references and local projections are highly original and have nothing in common with the literature from that period.

Las brujas is an opera that could be simply ruled an eccentric piece by an idealist who was rejected by society. However, the little we know about this work reveals a complex background. Perhaps, while he thought he had failed, the message Jiménez wished to transmit remains still hidden in the work.

The last letter known to have been penned by Jiménez, which he wrote shortly before dying, expresses his great disappointment with the rejection of his work and contains a last reflection on Rinaldo's character:

> . . . *deeply dejected by these recent events, I have decided not to write or feel music anymore; my old ideals of youth have, perhaps, made me think of myself as my character, who would eventually find redemption; but I don't expect this anymore, nor can I see the future, so I am merely content with entrusting my soul to God and finding peace in Heaven after so much scorn and so much torment.*

THE CONNECTICUT STORY

(1952)

Richard Pryce

Richard Pryce (1915–1978) was a composer born in Alabama. African-American and an orphan, he had an underprivileged childhood that only worsened in his teenage years during the Depression. According to a biographical note written for a musical publication, an aunt of his sent Pryce to Hoboken, New Jersey, where he would hold various jobs. Eventually he worked in New York's meat packing district and, later, for a wealthy family in Staten Island. It is thought that these early experiences may have inspired some of Pryce's characters in *The Connecticut Story*.

Pryce discovered music in the underground bars of Harlem, which were frequented by such historical jazz personalities as Duke Ellington and Billy Holliday. At around 1932, Pryce began to compose music for piano. Thanks to a mentor who recognized Pryce's talent, he was awarded a scholarship at the Curtis Institute of Music in Philadelphia—something unusual at that time, as no composers of color had ever attended that school. Pryce learned conducting and composition and became part of a generation of American composers that includes Ned Rorem, Samuel Barber (with whom he developed a particular friendship), and Leonard Bernstein. The influence of these composers, as that of Aaron Copland's, is clear in Pryce's dramatic lyricism, his affinity for the traditional melodic line, his orchestration style, and his effort to create a distinctly "American" piece. Unlike these composers, however, Pryce's professional life was much more complex and he was faced with numerous obstacles. The fact that he was a black musician in the usually conservative world of classical music deprived him of a number of opportunities that were available to his contemporaries. In the world of American music, African-Americans were relegated to the genres of blues and jazz, and were rarely considered for any roles in the classical music scene, except for that of lead singer. It was even more unusual for a black musician to be seriously regarded as a composer or to be offered the post of orchestra conductor. As a result, Pryce was forced to take several jobs that had nothing to do with music and, eventually, worked in the publishing section of the sheet music printer Karl Fischer & Co. It was through this job that he met the multifaceted and charismatic black singer Paul Robeson. Robeson took an interest in his work and, on one occasion, sang one of Pryce's early compositions, *Four Midnight Songs*, as a way to aid the young composer's career. The attention these pieces received led to some interesting commissions, including an operatic version of *The Glass Menagerie* by Tennessee Williams. While working on this project, Pryce developed an interest in Williams' dramatic forms, which would later influence his own work.

The Connecticut Story was originally commissioned by the American Opera Theater of New York, whose director, Elmer Brighton, was seeking to produce a new romantic drama. Brighton suggested that Pryce work on the project with the poet and librettist Earnest Reade Thomas. Thomas, a promising writer and recent graduate of Princeton, had become engaged in dramaturgy in a number of small productions at the time, and his apparent ease at writing elegant and emotionally-charged lyrics made Brighton think that Thomas would make a fitting collaborator for Pryce.

Indeed, while working together, Pryce and Thomas found many affinities with each other and, partly as a result of their intensive collaboration, they became romantically involved. This generated a complex situation due to the fact that Thomas was married. Even though the loud rumors about Thomas's bisexuality and his relationship with Pryce grew, Thomas never left his wife or disclosed his affair. Reade Thomas maintained his secret relationship with Pryce until the end of his life. It is evident from recently discovered letters between the two that the relationship was extremely passionate and that their intellectual and personal bond was unique, particularly in the case of Pryce, who never had another relationship or partner in his life.

Synopsis of the Opera

The piece takes place during World War II. Rick Robertson is an African-American hotel bellhop at the Grand Hotel Connecticut in Old Greenwich, Connecticut. Emily Jones, the owner of the luxurious hotel, is the last descendant of a New England aristocratic family. The racial and aristocratic stratification of that period is very clear in this first part of the opera. The following events, however, take an unexpected turn both within the opera and within the traditional war stories in American literature. In the second act, we witness a dystopian future in which the United States has lost the battle of Normandy and, as a result of a German-Japanese counterattack, an occupation of the American territory ensues. Several years later, Americans are second-class citizens in a divided country whose political and economic interests are administered by pro-occupation Americans, who watch over the interests of Japan, Russia, and Germany. In this dystopian future, the United States is not a world power but a country ravaged by war that has never recovered from the era of the Depression. It is a weak country largely suffering from the problems of the Third World.

Within this context, The Grand Hotel Connecticut is the last suburban landmark of aristocratic America, where Emily Jones tries to hide, until the end, the sad truth that Americans are living. Her hotel represents a sort of imaginary and ideal world that reflects the nostalgia for what America was or could have been. The hotel's guests are people with a similar background to Emily Jones'; they seek to maintain their old visions of lineage, power and influence within the confines of the magnificent hotel. Rick, who aside from his duties as a bellhop has also served Emily as a butler and somewhat of a family confidant, secretly desires Emily but could not even imagine insinuating it for the obvious reasons of the racial and social divide. Emily lives in a world of denial that is somewhat nurtured by Rick, whom she treats condescendingly, and is entirely oblivious to his devotion to her. Rick allows this treatment because he, always selfless, feels sorry for her situation and because of his secret feelings for her. At the same time, Emily becomes romantically involved with Mark Toyer, a shady investor whom Rick detests and suspects to be a mere opportunist.

Emily keeps up the hotel and her luxurious lifestyle through large debts that, in the end, become impossible to pay. As she becomes willing to do anything to maintain her way of life, she gradually allows Mark Toyer to handle her finances. Toyer takes advantage of this situation to run an even larger amount of debts in Emily's name without her full awareness; he talks Emily into securing loans and investments for the hotel using manipulated financial reports. This plan is eventually discovered by Rick, who accidentally overhears a conversation between them. In the meantime, Emily accidentally finds a picture of herself in Rick's room and is horrified to discover his feelings for her. In a confrontation between the two, their secrets come to light and Rick sees no other choice but to quit his job and leave the hotel.

Three years later, Jones' creditors and financial victims sue her and, despite her many appeals, she eventually loses her property, which will be demolished for the construction of an office building. Toyer flees the country and Emily is sentenced to ten years in prison.

Eventually, Emily is evicted but she refuses to leave her room in the heart of the building. Rick, who now lives in New York and has a prosperous job as the manager of a hotel in Harlem, hears about Emily's situation and decides to visit her.

The power relationships become reverted in the end, as we see a weak and frightened woman fall in the arms of a black man who is trying to reconcile his resentment toward his past and the strength he now possesses for having always been discriminated against by society.

As the building begins to be demolished, Rick tries to take Emily out, but she decides to remain inside—an act that constitutes suicide—rather than confronting the end of the Grand Hotel Connecticut.

Historical Context

Pryce's work was written during an anticlimactic and psychologically fragile time in the United States, as the country emerged triumphantly from the post-war period and entered the Cold War.

Consequently, this work was not appealing at all to the audiences or the critics of the time. Eventually, a group of McCarthist whistleblowers set their eyes on Pryce and concluded that his radical topics were attempting to spread communist ideology in the United States. Although Pryce was not prosecuted in the end, the communist accusations marred his reputation amongst the music community and contributed to haunt him over the years, preventing him from receiving other important professional opportunities.

In 1985, the historian Archibald Hayes, who was interested in the life and work of Pryce, was able to recover several of Pryce's manuscripts and wrote a biography of the composer titled *Richard Pryce: Out of Darkness*, which helped shed some light on the impact that Pryce's personal experiences, such as his relationship with Reade Thomas and his episode with the McCarthists, had on his musical work.

Critical Analysis of the Opera

Even though *The Connecticut Story* is a piece with dramatic forms and strategies that are consistent with the music and theater of its time, the work's subtext makes it stand out among the operatic production of post-war American music. We could definitely say, as Hayes has stated in his biographical study, that Pryce's racial and political experiences deeply shaped the character of his whole artistic production. It is particularly important to consider certain aspects of Pryce's life, such as his secret homosexual and biracial relationship with Reade Thomas, who was white. The relationship between the characters of Rick and Emily contains similar tensions: physical attraction and impossibility of intimacy caused by their difference in class and race. Certain aspects of Rick and Emily's relationship are at times on the verge of the preposterous (as observed by those who objected to the opera when the first scripts circulated before its production), but they also appear to illustrate Pryce's own love experiences, and strongly suggest that Pryce and Reade Thomas regarded this collaborative work as a testament of their own impossible affair.

The Connecticut Story is an opera about power relationships on the economic, political and sentimental levels. While the Grand Hotel Connecticut represents the arising state of optimistic self-deceit prevalent at that time, which now characterizes modern American society (and which Pryce brilliantly captured then), the relationship between Rick and Emily illustrates the class division that still exists in the United States today. With the opera's turn of events, of nearly biblical proportions, Pryce seems to glorify those who live in the lower strata of American society, something that probably comes from his childhood in the religious South. It is impossible to avoid comparing the work with Margaret Mitchell's pivotal 1936 novel *Gone With the Wind*, within the apocalyptic and racial setting created by Pryce. But, unlike this film and other operas composed in this period, the social and racial conflicts portrayed in *The Connecticut Story* are not only presented in a harsher way, but they simply have no possible solution. For this reason, it must have been difficult for the public to assimilate the opera's message. Pryce's opera precedes Bernstein's *West Side*

Story by more than five years, and it introduces dramatic elements and social issues that had never been used in American musical theater until then.

The Fate of *The Connecticut Story*

Due to the controversy surrounding its theme, this opera was never produced. Because of a previous agreement, The New York Opera Theater produced an earlier work of Pryce titled *Fanny's Birthday*, a one-act opera that lacked the political dimension of *The Connecticut Story*. Although Pryce publicly stated that this incident did not affect him and that he would continue composing, it is clear that the critics' rejection of *The Connecticut Story* made a major dent in his self-esteem. A couple of years later, Pryce produced another opera titled *Farmer's Market* at the D'Amato Opera on Manhattan's Lower East Side; this was his last cooperation with Reade Thomas. The critical reception of the opera was uneven.

Reade Thomas died in March of 1956—an incident that was very traumatic for Pryce. It is known that, by the time of Reade Thomas' death, certain animosity had emerged between Pryce and Reade Thomas' wife, to the extent that she asked him not to attend the funeral. It must have been a highly painful experience for the composer to mourn the death of the love of his life in private. Soon after, Pryce severed all of his professional relationships and friendships and moved to Chicago, where he lived a reclusive life as a music instructor at the Sherwood Conservatory of Music. Quite possibly, the death of Pryce's main source of creative and sentimental support made him decide to stop composing. However, this is not known with certainty as Pryce stopped writing letters. Reade Thomas was the only real recipient of his correspondence and, once Pryce stopped writing to him, there was no more information to gather.

By the early seventies, Pryce had been practically forgotten as a composer. But in 1974, after more than a decade of creative silence, he wrote *Three Spirituals*, a masterpiece that seems to indicate his return to the simple and spiritual life of the Deep South. At around that time, he was also commissioned a composition by the DuSable Museum of African Art. The resulting piece, titled *Isis Rises*, is about Egypt and explores ideas related to the Nation of Islam; this would be his last work. After many attempts and postponements, however, Pryce never completed it. He spent his last years struggling with debt and alcoholism. On August 4 of 1978, Pryce was found dead in a public restroom in Chicago's Union Station. In his raincoat pocket, he carried a train ticket to Greenwich, Connecticut.

JAHANNAM

(1989)

Mona Kassem

On April 5, 2004, in the middle of the production of a documentary, the video artist Mona Kassem went for a walk on the streets of Jerusalem with her camera. She was never seen again and no trace of her was ever found.

The strange disappearance of Kassem was the conclusion of a life full of turns that are as unusual as they are enigmatic. Kassem was born into a humble family in a mosque in Damascus in 1955. One of her sisters died in an accident. At a very young age, Kassem moved to Dearborn, Michigan (an immigrant Arab suburb near Detroit) with her family. In an interview, Kassem recalls that as a child she was taken to see *Turandot*, an experience that made her want to become an opera composer someday. In 1977, after finishing her studies in music and journalism at the University of Illinois in Champaign-Urbana, she went back to Damascus for the first time. That experience clearly had a great impact in her creative life and resulted in her first video: *Sometimes the Head of a Serpent*. During this trip, Kassem discovered her interest in electronic music and decided that she was not really interested in documentary journalism.

In 1978, Kassem moved to New York and almost immediately became involved with the East Village art scene. Several anecdotes about this time describe her intense personality, full of energy and drama. "Kassem was a striking woman," recalls Chantal Akerman, "tall and curvaceous, with long dark hair and penetrating eyes; she was one of those people who walks into place and immediately changes the atmosphere." Kassem had particularly special talents: she stood out among the East Village artists of the time because of her innate talent for musical composition and her innovative way of using the video camera.

Kassem's previous experience as a documentary filmmaker helped her produce her videos; one of them (*Weeper*) was shown at Art in General in 1982. From 1981 to 1984, Kassem worked as Nam June Paik's assistant, an experience that gave her the opportunity to interact with such composers and artists as Milton Babbitt, Lauri Anderson, Steven Reich, and Beryl Korot. In 1981 she also began her romantic relationship with Palestinian artist Shazia Challyn.

The works produced by Kassem during the eighties reveal influences of minimalism, electronic music, and elements derived from contemporary dance and performance art. In 1989, Challyn was caught in a crossfire near the Jerusalem border and, after several weeks in agony, she died. This incident was the origin of *Jahannam*. Kassem discussed that time in her life in a 1994 interview:

> . . . *up to that moment, I think I had kept a certain separation that I thought was normal, perhaps, between one's private and public life, spirituality, and political*

tendencies. All that fell apart with this incident. It made me realize that, from that moment on, I couldn't conceive the world without all of my actions, artistic or not, being perfectly consistent with my ideals, fears and indignations.

Kassem became especially known for her extremely controversial views against Israel and in favor of the Palestinian cause, a stance that became more aggressive in the following years; though it is also true that, over this same period, she turned more critical of religious Islamic fanaticism. Kassem's works were often filled with humor: in 1987, in part to criticize the West's excessive romanticism of Eastern spirituality, she developed a series of New Age workshops in which she taught meditation, spiritual exercises, and tantric movements that supposedly came from the ancient East but were completely fabricated. The workshops were immensely popular and all kinds of affluent people attended them, both from art circles and not. And when the public discovered that Kassem had invented these practices, a heated controversy ensued that actually did nothing but help increment Kassem's reputation as an artist. Kassem's controversial actions came to an end in 1994, however, when she staged a torture school for Israeli soldiers as part of an exhibit for the Whitney Museum. This caused the Zionist group of Manhattan to file a lawsuit against her. Also, and in light of the growing controversy, the officials at the Whitney Museum decided to close the exhibition and resorted to various legal maneuvers to detach themselves from the incident, something that left Kassem in a particularly vulnerable position. As a result, Kassem eventually left the United States for Europe. Her work for the Whitney Museum brought about a wave of criticism. Joan Smithson, for example, wrote for the *New York Times*:

> *Kassem tries to provoke and irritate the public with a piece that falls into the same practices she criticizes, like contradictory gibberish, without any major esthetic considerations but with the apparent assumption that her actions will enter the category of artistic magnificence.*

In a passionate letter she sent to *Artforum* magazine in 1996, which was never published, Kassem revealed her apparent disappointment with the art world and announced her decision to abandon her artistic practice altogether. In the letter, Kassem wrote that she had come to the realization that the art world was so irrevocably linked to economic and political interests that any type of real criticism or change was impossible. The accusatory tone of her letter meant a definite rupture with the art world she had belonged to since her arrival to New York at the beginning of the eighties:

> *. . . over a decade ago, I realized that by making art I could articulate my feelings and ideas in a way that was impossible through any other media; that I could be part of a world in which I felt my voice belonged, and that through collective dialogue, I would be able to influence the prevailing discourse of the spheres of power. But, the more urgent this mission became for me, the more I realized that the kind of analysis, debate and activism that prevails in art circles is a mere sham. The economic ties and the proximity to that power have domesticated us, sitting us at the rich man's table as the court's small dissenting buffoon or*

as a lap dog. I am not giving up art but, out of respect to my principles, I can't continue to consider the art world as a valid interlocutor.

Kassem moved to Amsterdam and cut off her relationship with the art scene, as she had promised. Ironically, the type of projects she worked on during that period, mostly political documentaries, ended up being the most sophisticated in art and in form. They contain a poetic subtext that reflects the mind and sensibility of a great artist, regardless of whether she considered them art or not. Some compare Kassem's "rupture" with the art world to Lygia Clark's similar comment at the end of her life—her only work would be her therapeutic activities, which were actually still seen as art. Was Kassem playing with this ambiguity? Whatever the answer may be, the fact is that she and the art world never crossed paths again, and considering the art world's fast amnesia during the nineties, she was never thought of again until her disappearance.

About the Opera

Jahannam (pronounced *Jah-hah'-nam*) is a piece with a simple storyline that contains images and phrases from the Koran and the Bible to describe hell. The Arabic term "gehenna," which is the literal translation of "fire," represents the rejection of the sovereignty of God in the Muslim tradition. According to some Muslim theologians, hell is not a permanent state but a temporary condition akin to purgatory or limbo. The root of the word comes from the Hebrew *Gehinnom*, which is the name of a valley in the south of Jerusalem that has been used as a dump by the Israelis. In pre-Israelite times, the Canaanites worshiped a god named Moloch and sacrificed children in that valley, burning them as an offering to their deity (something of significance in this work, as the main character is a young girl). As a result, the valley has long been associated with fires and everything negative. According to the Koran, only God knows who will go to *Jahannam* and who will go to *Jannah*, as in the case of Judaism and Calvinism. All of those who don't believe in Allah will remain in *Jahannam* until the *Qiyamah* (Day of Judgment).

Jahannam uses Christian and Muslim words to recount in a symbolical way the historical conflict between both cultures and the consequences of that conflict, which have created what in both religions is considered a state of spiritual denial.

Synopsis of the Opera

Jahannam is structured more in the form of an oratorio than a dramatic opera or musical theater piece, as is the case with many operas by Philip Glass and Steve Reich. The narrative, which is relatively abstract and follows a "stream-of-consciousness" format, explores the experiences of Sefa, a Palestine girl who lives in the Israeli town of Jahannam, a frontier territory with Palestine settlements allowed by the Israelis. Sefa's father, the town's martyr, died a year before after being tortured by an Israeli soldier. Sefa corresponds with her cousin, whose family has immigrated to California and has a prosperous life there; the action is revealed to us through their letters.

Following a terrorist attack in Tel Aviv, which the Israelis attribute to a group of men who live in Jahannam, the town is surrounded by several bulldozers and tanks. The Israeli soldiers demand that these men surrender immediately and threaten to demolish the town unless their demand is met. A fence is kept up for several days, which causes many people to become injured. In the meantime, Sefa finds a wounded Israeli soldier under a bridge in Jahannam and realizes that, if she lets her people know about him, the soldier will be killed by the Palestinians. So she initiates a conversation with him and secretly brings him food and water, and a sort of friendship begins. Soon, though, Sefa finds out through the wounded soldier's stories that he is none other than the man who killed her father. After recovering from her initial shock, Sefa is torn between keeping her discovery a secret and revealing the soldier's hideout. Finally, she chooses the latter and the soldier is executed by the Palestinians. The opera ends as the Israeli bulldozers destroy the town and Sefa and her family die.

Much like a Palestinian *Ann Frank's Diary*, *Jahannam* is a sort of child's journal in which the tensions of the Palestinian-Israeli conflict are described.

Critical Analysis of the Opera

Kassem wrote *Jahannam* toward the end of the eighties, and around the fall of the Berlin Wall. The work has a predictably political side and, perhaps, shares some of the aspects of other works created during that period. However, *Jahannam*'s musical and formal turns make it a remarkable work within musical minimalism.

In 1996, Kassem wrote a very personal text about this opera, where she stated that she considered *Jahannam* her most ambitious work:

> *Regardless of whether Jahannam is a failure or not, the work contains, without a doubt, all of my ideas and inner conflicts, my personal moments, my questions; they are all situated across from one another, not always in a coherent manner. I only know that*

if there is something I would have liked to say in life, it is definitely there and the public can take it or leave it.

Jahannam contains four melodic sequences that alternate with one another, and accompany an account that comes from a specific moment in time. Three of those voices belong to the past, present, and future, respectively. The fourth is a timeless voice that we could say is the divine voice, and pronounces most of the quotations from the Koran and the Old Testament.

Perhaps, the difference between *Jahannam* and other works with the same themes is that, ultimately, Kassem, who considered herself a pro-Palestine activist, expresses her deep inner conflicts with respect to her own tradition and the Muslim beliefs. The division between Arabs and Israelis is a battle that takes place not among different people, but within each one of the characters in the work. Thus, the opera does not have an ethical or accusatory character—in fact, of all of Kassem's works, *Jahannam* is the least direct in her political message—, but simply a tone of stoic acceptance of a society's spiritual and historical contradictions. This aspect of the opera was not really appreciated by those who saw it at the time, perhaps because there is no room for ambivalence in the political climate of the Palestinian-Israeli conflict.

We should also remember that Kassem lived in the United States at the time and was probably going through a particular conflict regarding her upbringing, her origins, and her place between two realities. Kassem was educated in the calm Midwest and was tired of both the cultural stereotypes and the romantic perception the immigrant Arab community had of their home countries. This type of cultural tension can be clearly seen in the opera, both in the benevolent, romantic, and naïve melody that accompanies Sefa's cousin's voice, as in the disturbing music that accompanies Sefa's accounts of the atrocities she witnesses. In this work, Kassem deals with a variety of opposites, not only the Israeli and Palestinian cultures, but philosophical opposites as well—faith and pragmatism, past and present, friend and foe—which, in the end, are nothing more than the opposing voices within herself. Her apparent conclusion, as presented in the opera, is that these confrontations have no possible solution other than accepting a way of life that allows this permanent conflict to exist. Toward the end of *Jahannam*, Sefa's character says:

> *Father used to say that what happens to us in life doesn't matter because, in the end, we will all be with Allah in paradise. I never liked it when he said that. What would happen if there was suddenly no paradise? Sometimes I think that it is better to think there is no such better place; that this is the best place, even with all the sad things that happen in it . . . ; that this is paradise. And when I think this way, I feel better and can go to sleep.*

IL PROCESSO
DI GIORDANO BRUNO

(1898)

Enrico Camorelli

Enrico Camorelli was born in Naples, Italy, in 1868 and died in Milan in 1904, when he was 35 years old. His brief career took place during a golden moment of the Italian opera, when the Verismo style and the works by Giacomo Puccini prevailed. The child of an affluent liberal family, and famous for his looks and charisma, Camorelli's life was deeply influenced by Romanticism, and as a result of this influence, he saw music as a revolutionary act. Other early experiences would determine his view of the world in a significant way: as a child, he attended a seminary and this resulted in a strong disdain for religion, a feeling that can be perceived in many of his works. At the seminary, however, he also learned how to play the organ rather precociously and his interest in musical composition was born. It is said that by twelve years old he had memorized Bach's *The Well-Tempered Clavier* (*Das Wohltemperirte Clavier*) and played it impeccably, to his teachers' astonishment.

Camorelli's colleagues described him as an extremely intelligent man, obsessed with reason, Leibniz's pre-logic, and mathematics. He could read and memorize entire philosophical treatises in a few hours and was fascinated with the relationship between geometry and art, a connection that he was always searching for in nature and science. At 19 years old, he wrote a *Tractatus Mathematicus*, in which he tried to demonstrate this relationship. As a good philosopher and abstract thinker, Camorelli was known for being messy and absent-minded. And despite being full of idealistic and never-ending projects, he never completed his studies at the University of Bologna, where he began to study philosophy and later switched to music. Of particularly significance during his musical training were his studies in Paris, around 1886, with French composer César Franck. He and Franck shared an interest in the organ repertoire as well as a deep admiration for Bach's work. During that period, Franck had just finished composing one of his masterpieces, *Prèlude, Choral et Fugue* (1884) which, without a doubt, had a big influence in Camorelli's life.

In spite of his enormous talent, however, Camorelli never shared any of his compositions with anyone. He would spend endless hours writing music in his study, but his obsession with perfection made him destroy his manuscripts almost immediately after finishing them with a fury and violence that became infamous—his frequent outbursts were dreaded by his neighbors. During one of these fits, Camorelli is said to have thrown his piano from his balcony, killing a horse that was passing by on the street below. "Camorelli was ruthlessly strict with himself," says historian Anselm Gross, "he was so demanding with his own work that completing a piece became an impossible task and caused him great suffering, to the point of tears, as if it were a case of unrequited love." Camorelli became known among his friends for his legendary ability to improvise music and for his constant talk of the various compositions he was always working on, and their theoretical connection with a variety of philosophical and mathematical ideas. No one ever thought that he would actually finish a piece and, understandably, some might have even considered him a charlatan.

By 1899, Camorelli had apparently stopped composing (or trying to, at least) and was traveling around the Middle East on a "spiritual journey." In 1903, while in Algeria, Africa, he fell ill (apparently with malaria). He was bedridden for months and the illness led to his early death.

It was shortly after his death that, while packing up Camorelli's studio, one of his friends found, among the composer's private papers, a mysterious red velvet folder with the Tetragrammaton (the Hebrew word for God) symbol on its cover. (This revealed that Camorelli had converted to Judaism several years before.) Inside the folder was the manuscript for a completed opera.

Il processo di Giordano Bruno (The Trial of Giordano Bruno) was written between 1894 and 1898, and brought together what until then had been Camorelli's three passions: philosophy, mathematical logic, and music.

For some strange reason, not only did Camorelli never publish *Il processo di Giordano Bruno*, but he never told anyone about its existence either. While the most logical assumption is that he was not happy with the finished work (as had apparently always been the case), the fact that he had kept it indicates a certain attachment to the piece. According to Irmo Vacchianti, a close friend of his, Camorelli probably intended to leave this work up to fate, so future generations could find it. This is consistent with the composer's perception of his time and his own identification with Bruno, another misunderstood personality of that period. In a letter to his friend, Camorelli wrote:

> . . . *even if I vanished now, dear Irmo, I think I have left enough seeds that will show everything I have fought for and will redeem in art what I, perhaps, was not able to redeem throughout the actions of my life.*

Whatever the case, the truth is that even when the opera was discovered, little attention was paid to it for over a decade, until Vacchianti persuaded the printer Giulio Ricordi to publish it in 1917. It is known that *Il processo* was performed once in Genoa in 1925, but soon after fell into oblivion until 1960, when Franco Corelli recorded an aria from the opera and the work was redis-covered by the critics. Michael Donnington, the author of *Opera and Its Symbols* (1990), did a brilliant analysis of Camorelli's work. In it, he claims that *Il processo* con-tains a complex mix of symbols that are very consistent with the work of Bruno, who is thought to have written Hermetic texts disguised as mnemonic treatises.

Synopsis of the Opera

As its name indicates it, this opera is based on the famous 1593 trial by the Vatican of philosopher and oc-cultist Giordano Bruno. During the trial, which began in Venice and ended in Rome seven years later, Bruno was condemned for his spiritual ideas, his beliefs in Copernicus' perception of the universe (that the earth was not its center), and the notion that the universe was not exclusively limited by a celestial sphere. Bruno argued that the universe was formed by four unique elements (earth, water, air, and fire) and, based on this principles, had developed a complex Hermetic cosmogony.

Il processo opens in Oxford, England, where the first great cosmogonic debate took place between Bruno and his critics (George Abbott, Canterbury's archbishop, and John Underhill, Oxford's archbishop). In this debate, Bruno presents his radical ideas and questions himself about the beginning of the universe and its mechanisms.

In the second act, Bruno is visited one night by an anonymous character who seems to be a spirit (we don't know whether the spirit is evil or divine). Then, night after night, and using the ancient art of memory, this character dictates to Bruno the complex keys to divine and cosmic knowledge. Bruno spends months in his room, feverishly writing down his visitor's dictation. On the last night, his secret visitor gives Bruno the last key to the system but warns him that there will be serious consequences if he reveals the information to humanity. That's how Bruno ends his long treatise, titled *De umbris idearum* (The Shadow of Ideas)[2].

In the third act, a nomadic Bruno is this time in Paris, involved again in endless debates with the intellectuals of his time. In light of these debates, Bruno decides it is crucial that he make the recently-published *De umbris idearum* known to the world, despite the consequences.

Meanwhile, his so-called friend, the aristocratic Giovanni Mocenigo, invites him to Venice so Bruno can teach him the art of memory. But Mocenigo, who has been secretly jealous of Bruno's professional accomplishments for a long time, has set him a trap. When Bruno arrives in Venice, he is apprehended and he finds out that Mocenigo has reported his "heretic" ideas to the Inquisition.

---

2   In the original *De umbris idearum*, Bruno's ghostly interlocutor is Hermes.

During his long trial, Bruno tries to find a way to justify his ideas without contradicting the church's dogma, but he refuses to deny his belief in a multitude of worlds and the universe's infinity. Afterward, while already in prison, Bruno is visited once more by his ghostly interlocutor, who reprimands him for revealing these divine secrets and confirms that he will be sentenced to death. Bruno knows what is in store for him, but is determined to meet his fate without denying his beliefs.

In this opera's most famous aria, *Le sfere luminose* (The Luminous Sphere), Bruno has a last spiritual vision of eternity right before being burned at the stake.

The opera seems to end here, but *Il processo* is not a conventional piece in any sense. Instead of creating a predictable ending, Camorelli inserts a fourth act that has generated much discomfort, confusion and comment among historians and musicologists. While in the first act Camorelli uses dramatic forms and styles that are typical of an opera of that period, these conventions disappear in the fourth act and the public suddenly finds itself in an abstract moment in time (definitely a remote future), in which two contemporary characters—apparently not actors but academics—begin to debate, first, Giordano Bruno's ideas, then the actors' performances, and, finally, Camorelli's own beliefs!

For those familiar with Italian Verismo, the closest example to this scene is the appearance of Taddeo at the beginning of *Pagliacci* (*Si puo?* . . . *Si puo?* . . .) when, in an unprecedented dramatic gesture that breaks with the fourth wall act, the character addresses the audience to remind them that actors are human beings with real emotions. In the case of *Il processo*, however, Camorelli goes beyond that brief digression and, not only breaks the sacred threshold of dramatic fiction, but he opens in front of the audience what could be described as the Pandora's box of interpretation. The opera, about a human being (Bruno) who functions as an interpreter of the universe's divine vision, diverts into a reflection on the way in which the character of Bruno itself is interpreted by Camorelli; about the way in which the opera is interpreted by the singers (the interpreters); and, finally, the way in which all of these interpretative levels will be analyzed in the future by us.

In perspective, the discussion that takes place on stage seems to consist of what, at that time, were the debates among the faith advocates and the intellectuals of the end of the nineteenth century: some question Bruno's sanity and his communication with hell, while others justify him as a science martyr—something that, perhaps, Camorelli naively identified himself with, as could be expected of an artist who was still in his twenties.

Critical Analysis of the Opera

In this opera prima, Enrico Camorelli reveals a surprising command of orchestration, which places him at the level of such composers as Wagner and Meyerbeer. Unlike the Verismo-style operas of the time, however, *Il processo* contains rhythmic intervals that suddenly abandon their lyricism to acquire an orchestral atonality and complexity that were unheard of at that time, and would only be seen years later in Stravinsky's *The Rite of Spring* (1913). The fact that this opera was created by such a young composer, and that it was his only creation, is truly impressive. Most critical studies, however, agree that the piece suffers from certain excesses caused mostly by an extensive and elaborate libretto which, again, shows a great talent that had little experience with piecing together melody and ideas.

That said, it is unfair to consider this opera based on the simple and conventional esthetic parameters of this period, simply because *Il processo* is much more than an opera. Michael Donnington has been quoted as saying that Camorelli considered his work a "great fable or allegory, at once rational and contradictory, of the notion of interpretation, be it artistic, divine or both." Though somewhat skeptically, Camorelli was absolutely fascinated by the idea of the artist as a demiurge, elf of the forest, or divine entity that reveals unusual truths about the mortal world. Within this context, the opera's storyline, biographies and music are nothing more than simple vehicles to express certain comparative ideas about subjects that concerned the author at the time, as it is expressed in the third and fourth acts. These ideas come to a close in the last act, like a perfectly round hermetic universe. Camorelli created a character based on a real person named Giordano Bruno and, through fiction, was able to express his thoughts about that period. But, besides that, Camorelli created characters who questioned his own beliefs. And he created a last layer of uncertainty by introducing a character named Enrico Camorelli, who questions the veracity and the logic of everything that was expressed in the opera written by Enrico Camorelli. In a moment typical of Borges, we are lost in Camorelli's work, which is paradoxically the perfect expression of the central premise of Giordano Bruno's masterpiece: the world is a system of secret references, where we can only see the shadows of ideas. What will reveal the truth to us is our ability to interpret them and relate them correctly—and perhaps that truth lies only within the multiplicity that exists within ourselves, the most familiar and yet most foreign territory we can penetrate. That was probably the very essence of the divine knowledge that eluded both Bruno and Camorelli.

FUGUE (AND VARIATION)

Unlike other forms of visual art, the presentation of an opera entails a variety of elements that make its study particularly complex. These elements can be divided into two categories: the strictly formal aspects of the genre—such as musical composition, libretto, and staging—and the strictly interpretative aspect. A key difference between opera and the visual arts genre, for example, is the codependency between the composer and the interpreter. Since the singer, or musician, makes a composition come to life, it becomes difficult, if not impossible, to pinpoint what aspect of the interpretation is the result of the composer's vision versus the musician's vision. It can be said that the composer's view becomes visible through the composite memories of its many interpreters but, when focusing on each unique interpretation, the range of creative possibilities in interpreting the performance of the work is so large that they can be regarded, at the very least, as a form of collaboration.

How could one approach a comparison between such different operas and, above all, such different composers as a *mestizo* from colonial Mexico, a lesbian Arab video artist who was involved in the East Village scene of the eighties, a turn-of-the-century Italian dandy, and a gay African-American composer of the Cold War era? I will not try to uncover magical connections between these works or composers but, instead, I will simply try to point out the relationships between these pieces through the model of the four-voice fugue.

The contrapuntal form of the fugue, which in the West reached its peak with the work of J.S. Bach, consists of the introduction of at least three voices, and up to eight or nine, each one developing a theme that is reproduced by the following voice. Next, I will describe the format of a four-voice fugue:

The first voice establishes what is known as a formal *exposition* of the *subject* (main melody). It is followed by a freer section, generally called *development*, which ends with a *recapitulation* that goes back to the *subject* in the same key as it began and concludes more emphatically. The second voice, known as *answer*, enters the scene once the first voice has presented the subject, and develops on its own following the format of the first voice. Then the third voice appears, generally presenting what is known as the *countersubject*. The countersubject is a melodic idea that consistently appears with the subject during the exposition, as well as further along the fugue. The third voice or countersubject must be melodically interesting, have individuality and enough rhythmic contrast to successfully accompany the subject. As the expert George Oldroyd accurately says: "They must have been made for each other."[3] In addition, the *countersubject* and the *subject* must be interchangeable, that is to say, each one must function well as a high-pitch or a low-pitch voice. Likewise, the fourth voice must complement the second voice just as the third voice complements the first voice.

In the majority of four-voice contrapuntal compositions, not all voices are included all the time, for it is difficult for the ear to follow four melodies of equal importance and complexity for long periods of time. Therefore, one or two melodies usually disappear every once in a while to add variety to the texture of the work.

---

3 George Oldroyd, *The Technique and Spirit of Fugue* (London: Oxford University Press, 1948; p. 38)

Given that we can create four types of fugues at this point, we will complete four comparative exercises in this study:

I.   Musically: Using elements of the different compositions to create a fugue.

II. Visually: Generating simultaneous views of one scene of each opera (four images with one stage set each, as the four operas have four sections or acts).

III. Interpretatively: Alternating comments by critics of each work: historians, researchers, or the composers themselves.

IV. Textually: Alternating different phrases and texts from each one of the librettos (in English first and in their original languages after).

Based on the typical order of the voices in a fugue, as used by Bach in *The Well-Tempered Clavier*, the fourth section will have the following format:

1234
4321
2143
2341
3214
3412 (bis)

I.

Las brujas de Tepoztlán—Introduction to the first act (*Salve Regina*)

Il processo di Giordano Bruno—Fourth act aria (*Le sfere luminose*)

The Connecticut Story—Emily's aria, third act

Jahannam—End

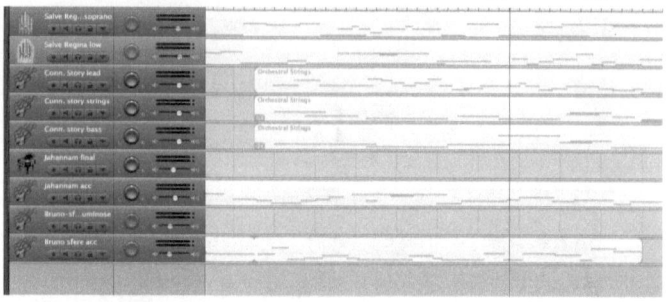

Recording of the four previous pieces

II.

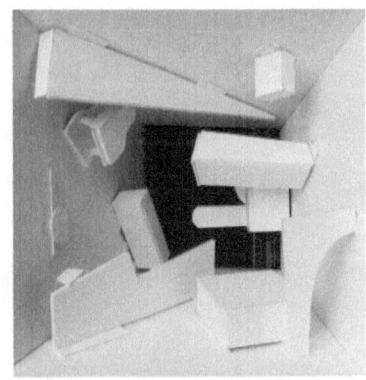

Four stage sets, each one corresponding to the first act of each opera (from upper left to lower right): *Jahannam* (Jahannam's dump); *The Connecticut Story* (Emily's piano room); *Las brujas de Tepoztlán* (a street in the center of town); *Il processo di Giordano Bruno* (a square in Oxford in Renaissance England)

III.

[Given: 1 = *The Connecticut Story*; 2 = *Las brujas de Tepoztlán*; 3 = *Jahannam*; 4 = *Il processo di Giordano Bruno*; and a = Richard Pryce; b = Anselmo Jiménez de la Rueda; c = Mona Kassem d = Enrico Camorelli]

1^2^3^4. This piece deals with the clash of cultural identities during a historical period of crises and political unrest. The human dilemmas presented in the work are metaphors for identity problems, some of them of a meta-historical nature.

1^2^3^4. In the piece, the characters experience an unexpected revelation or epiphany (of either personal or spiritual nature) that reveals truths that take them into action. This revelation transforms and completes the characters, but its knowledge also causes new problems, like a fulfilled wish that carries fatal consequences.

1^4. The main character is subjected to a trial during which his main wishes and values are questioned. The character is sentenced at the end of the trial but refuses to change his or her perception of reality.

2^3. The main character seems to be in a position to condemn others, acting as a judge in an uncontrollable reality. In one way or another, in the end the character's verdict will harm him or herself.

1^2. The main characters are able to see something—either the future or an illusion—that is invisible to others.

1^3. The characters confront a destructive world that they would prefer did not exist, but it eventually becomes their reality.

1^3. The protagonists become deeply rooted to their place of origin, as if losing it meant losing their most profound identity, and cannot imagine abandoning it. This will have serious consequences.

1^3. There is a reversion of roles among the characters: the one in power becomes defeated while the oppressed suddenly finds him or herself in a position of power and has the possibility of taking some kind of revenge.

1^4. The protagonists are subjected to trial by a society that, until that moment, has acted as their interlocutor and whose severity will fall hard on their destinies.

2^3. In this work, there is a confusion of identities that proves fatal for one of the characters in the plot.

2^4. The protagonist is an idealist who has a vision of the afterlife—a unique vision that gives him clarity but also separates him from reality.

2^4. The protagonist ends up achieving what he was looking for, but the fulfillment of this wish has fatal consequences.

4^3. The work seems to criticize religious intolerance and dogmatism, and the type of ridiculous or tragic actions these beliefs can cause us to take.

4^3. The characters perceive a divine order in the universe but that certainty causes nothing but frustration, for they live in an unequal and chaotic world that does not conform to those ideals at all. The characters' negotiation of these two contradictory worlds becomes the central conflict in the action.

1^2^3. The characters live in an atmosphere of tension because of their social class or ethnicity which, though not expressly articulated, is the subtext of the action and informs the type of decisions they make.

a^b^c^d. The composer's life experiences with regards to his or her social condition can be seen in the work; the composer feels different to others, or has been rejected by society. This peculiarity that turns him or her into both spectator and judge of others is reflected in several of the characters.

a^b^c^d. The author was misunderstood as was his or her work, which was destined to survive destiny's twists and turns and reach our time. Only then was the work appreciated as a visionary testament to the period in which it was written.

b^d. Magic and the occult play an important role in the life of the composer and these elements are symbolically revealed in the work.

c^d. The composer is driven by a wish to transform society and constantly becomes involved in big projects that include trips abroad, an activity that eventually brings about his or her own death.

a^b. The composer is a timid person whose personality has, without a doubt, contributed to his not being recognized during his lifetime and falling into oblivion.

a^c. The death of the composer's lover is a decisive event in his or her life and is intrinsically related to his or her creativity.

IV.

(English version)

EMILY
What a beautiful spring morning! The birds are flowing back from winter. I wish I could do the same, go
elsewhere and come back.

RINALDO
Beautiful Dorotea, daughter of dawn, marvelous light,
Listen to me with all your love and, now,
Look at this poor heart that writhes in pain.

SEFA
It's early here today and we haven't seen any soldiers yet.
My mother makes a run for water now—she says this
    is the safest time of the day.

MOCENIGO
The stars hide tonight, the sky is black
But I feel their shining in my soul.
When shall I know their mystery?

BRUNO
The universe is as eternal and infinite as God
No one other than the stars
Can write the future of every thing;
We are letters from the divine book.

WALID

The day that He assembles you all for a day of assembly—that will be a day of mutual loss and gain among you. Those who believe in Allah and work righteousness, He will remove from their ills, and He will admit them to gardens beneath which rivers flow, to dwell therein for ever: that will be the Supreme Achievement.

RINALDO

Witch, sorceress, highest magician of the cave;
Help me forget my heart's delirium,
For my mind can no longer survive,
This passion will kill me with anxiety;
Return my happiness, my simple life, to me
And let whatever I lose be my gain.

EMILY

I don't want to talk about it, Rick. I want to think
That all is exactly the same as it ever was.
What is the point of living in the present, when
You can be happy living in the past?

RINALDO

How is this possible?
What sort of science is this?
My eyes can see beyond our time,
One hundred, two hundred years?
I see the valley of Mexico
Amongst shades of gray,
Hundreds of buildings like mountains,
Pyramidal, infinite, on earth.
Thousands of men inhabit them,
Moving violently to and fro.
Mechanisms of iron and glass

Surround every corner
Like the wind,
Great mobile machines in a race;
Is this the city of my tomorrow?
How will we reach this tragic hell?
What sins will we commit, my Lord,
To fall to the bottom of that dark abyss?

RICK
I often ask myself: why is it that one should suffer in love,
How is it that we so easily fall in the dark fire of desire,
That hopeless pit where there is no way out,
Why are we born to want that which is impossible to attain,
Why do I suffer, Oh Lord, if I have done nothing wrong,
What penance am I paying, to want something that I
     will never get?

BRUNO
In every object there is an idea
Inside every idea there is a shadow
A dark shadow that is the mirror
Of the infinite and the depths
Within which we find the truth,
The greatest truth of all
That can be found: the secret of the universe.

WALID
Sefa, I am fighting for our freedom, and these people
want to take it away from you. I am here to protect you.
They want a future without us, but we have a right to
a future too.

They see the Day indeed as a far-off event, but we see
it quite near. The Day that the sky will be like molten

brass, and the mountains will be like wool, and no friend will ask after a friend, though they will be put in sight of each other, the sinner's desire will be that he could redeem himself from the penalty of that day by sacrificing his children, his wife and his brother, his kindred who sheltered him, and all, all that is on earth, so it could deliver him: by no means! For it would be the Fire of Hell! Plucking out (his being) right to the skull! Inviting all such as turn their backs and turn away their faces.

RINALDO
My Lord! It is me! Me in my tomb!
And my beloved Dorotea with Torrijos.
Oh no, that will not be my future,
To die without children, or love, or mourning!
To face nothingness!
I won't let heaven do that,
And Torrijos shall not outlive me unscathed;
He will taste my sword.

SEFA
And then I saw the wounded man, hiding under the bridge. He couldn't move. The men from my neighborhood came in the morning looking for him, but I knew that if I told them where he was, they would kill him.

IL GIUDICE
Do you rebuff your affirmation that the universe is infinite; that it consists of an immense ethereal region; that that sun, the moon and countless other bodies exist in this ethereal region; that it is not to be believed that there is a firmament?

BRUNO

You may judge me thinking you have the divine power; but that divine power exists in every object and every living human being. How could I renounce what I know is true, what I know to be the fundamental law of the universe? Judges, beware of your verdict, because you shall be judged in the same manner!

EMILY

Rick, don't leave, please. I need you. I need your strength with me.

RICK

Miss Emily ... there is nothing I can do for you.

EMILY

You resent me, don't you? You do, don't you?

RICK

I never existed for you. I was invisible. You only see me now because you are weak, because you are confused. But it doesn't matter, because I can't do anything about it. I wish I could. I really do.

EMILY

I just want you to be with me. Please don't treat me the way I have treated you ...

RICK

The time has come, Miss Emily, it is time for you to leave. We have to leave.

SEFA

Walid says that we have to leave Jahannam tomorrow;
that it is not safe for us to be here. But we cannot leave.
My mother wonders what good it is for them to leave
their only home, what the point is.

WALID

But those who reject Faith and treat our signs as false-
hoods, they will be companions of the fire, to dwell
therein for aye: and evil is that goal. No kind of calamity
can occur, except by the leave of Allah: and if anyone
believes in Allah, Allah guides his heart: for Allah knows
all things. So obey Allah, and obey His Apostle: but if
ye turn back, the duty of Our Apostle is but to proclaim
the Message clearly and openly.

RINALDO

All I can do is wait now. Tonight will be your last, Torrijos,
And after piercing your treacherous body with my sword,
A vague memory you'll become,
And when your deep eyes become still,
Mine will own Dorotea, and only she they will love.

EL COMENDADOR

I silently walk in, for I wish to surprise Torrijos
With the news of my decision.
When my daughter marries him,
A new son I will have
And a distinguished position.

RINALDO

Beware! Those are steps I hear. Time to attack.
(*Rinaldo stabs El Comendador*)
Now die, you wretched man!

EL COMENDADOR
By Christ! You've wounded me, Rinaldo.

RINALDO
Comendador! How did this happen?
Oh no! Hell, please take me!
(*enter Torrijos and Dorotea*)

TORRIJOS
What is this ruckus I hear in my house?
What do I see? Rinaldo has stabbed your father!
I will catch you, you scoundrel, for my mother!
(*Torrijos wounds Rinaldo*)

DOROTEA
Stop, Torrijos! Oh, Virgin Mary! That wound!
What have my eyes seen?
My love falls, bleeding, and with him my life.

EMILY
This place is my life, and I am part of it,
We shall never be apart. If it falls, may I fall with it.
If I were to leave with the wound, it will never heal.
I cannot conceive any other life, or any other place.

RICK
This is crazy, you cannot let yourself perish.

EMILY
It is too late to be reborn. I have played my cards, and
I have lost.

LO SPIRITO

You broke the rule. You sought to reveal the hidden truths. For that, you will have to bear the consequences. You were given a special gift, the key to understanding the world. I showed you a glimpse of Paradise, but you squandered this knowledge. You were given God's knowledge, but you pretended to exercise it as if you were God. You may say you know the truth, but others will not listen, will not understand; it will be as though you spoke to them in another language. Knowledge brings solitude.

BRUNO

You've taught me that, like the universe, we are all a multiplicity of beings, a multiplicity of voices, ruled by the four cardinal winds. Each one of our voices provides a key to our understanding. Grant me those insights, allow me to see and understand beyond myself and my humble body, beyond my doubts and my fears; let me gaze beyond the shores of humanity that are contained within myself; allow me to see light in the darkness, the divine light that emerges from the shadows, the divine light that emerges from the shadows.

WALID

Your riches and your children may be but a trial: but the presence of Allah is the highest reward. So fear Allah as much as ye can; listen and obey and spend in charity for the benefit of your own soul and those saved from the covetousness of their own souls—they are the ones that will achieve prosperity.

If ye give to Allah a bountiful loan, He will double it to your credit, and He will grant you forgiveness: for Allah is most forbearing . . .

BRUNO

I fought, and that was difficult. I thought I could win . . .
but nature and luck have curbed my endeavor. It's already
something that I took up the struggle, because I see that
victory is in the hands of Fate. Within me was what was
possible and what no one can deny to me: everything a
winner could give of himself; that I did not fear death,
that I was always strong, and that I did not submit to
anyone of my breed; that I have preferred courageous
death to a passive life . . . I cleave the heavens, and soar
to the infinite. What others see from afar, I leave far
behind me.

EMILY

I will finally be able to fly and get away from the winter.

RINALDO

Dorotea, I will die happy knowing I am loved.

SEFA

I don't like to think there is a better place than this.

BRUNO

Unless you make yourself equal to God, you shall not
understand God, for the like is not intelligible except
to the like. Make yourself grow to a greatness beyond
measure, free yourself from the confines of your body,
raise yourself above all time, become Eternity; then you
will be able to understand God. Believe that nothing is
impossible for you, think of yourself immortal and ca-
pable of understanding everything, all arts, all sciences,
and the nature of every human being. Fly higher than
the highest height and descend lower than the lowest
depth. Feel within yourself the sensations of everything

created, fire and water, dry and moist, imagining that your soul is everywhere, on earth and in the sea, in the sky; that you are not yet born, you are in your mother's womb, adolescence, old age, death, beyond death. If you embrace your thoughts and everything at once: the times, places, substances, and quantities, you may understand God.

Oh luminous spheres,
Oh keepers of the truths and secrets of nature,
You are the ladder with which nature descends to the
    creation of all things
And with which the intellect ascends to the knowl-
    edge of them,
With it, ones and others shall return to unity.

EMILY
In life, we build castles that slowly wash away, in death, we wash away and a castle is built upon us . . .

RINALDO
My soul will leave now, my wakefulness is over.
I've lived a miserable life, but I die content.
I've seen the truth on earth and in heaven.
My love, never consummated, was real,
And I know that once gone,
My memory will not be lost;
It will endure, like ivy,
And will name each shadow and each stone.
You in me, and I in all of you,
A spell from Tepoztlán made me go wrong
But in my mistakes I found wisdom,
And it will be they who reveal the truth
So others who come to earth
Are able to read between the lines of life.

IV.

(Original version)

EMILY
What a beautiful spring morning! The birds are flowing back from winter. I wish I could do the same, go elsewhere and come back.

RINALDO
Hermosa Dorotea, hija de la aurora, divino resplandor,
Oídme con vuestro amor y, ahora
Observa este pobre corazón que se vuelca de dolor.

SEFA
It's early here today and we haven't seen any soldiers yet.
My mother makes a run for water now—she says this
    is the safest time of the day.

MOCENIGO
Le stelle si nascondono stanotte, il cielo è nero,
Ma sento il loro fulgore nell' anima.
Quando mi direte il vostro segretto?

BRUNO
L'universo è eterno ed infinito come Dio,
Nessun'altro che le stelle
Scrive il futuro di ogni cosa
Siamo lettere dal testo divino.

WALID

The day that He assembles you all for a day of assembly—that will be a day of mutual loss and gain among you. Those who believe in Allah and work righteousness, He will remove from their ills, and He will admit them to gardens beneath which rivers flow, to dwell therein for ever: that will be the Supreme Achievement.

RINALDO

Bruja, hechicera, maga suprema de la cueva;
Hazme olvidar los delirios de mi corazón,
Que mi mente no puede ya vivir entera,
Por esta pasión que me ha de matar por ansia,
Devolvedme mi felicidad, mi vida austera,
Y que lo que yo pierda sea mi ganancia.

EMILY

I don't want to talk about it, Rick. I want to think
That all is exactly the same as it ever was.
What is the point of living in the present, when
You can be happy living in the past?

RINALDO

Pero cómo, ¿qué ciencia es esta?
Mis ojos ven más allá del tiempo,
¿Cien, doscientos años?
Veo al valle de México
En colores grisáceos,
Cientos de edificios como montañas
Piramidales, infinitos, de la tierra,
Miles de hombres la habitan en andar violento,
Artificios de cristal y de hierro
Rodean cada esquina, y como el viento
Grandes máquinas movibles en carrera ...

¿Es esta la ciudad de mi mañana?
¿Como llegaremos a ese infierno trágico,
¿Qué pecados, Dios mío, cometeremos
para caer tan al fondo de ese negro precipicio?

RICK

I often ask myself: why is it that one should suffer in love,
How is it that we so easily fall in the dark fire of desire,
That hopeless pit where there is no way out,
Why are we born to want that which is impossible to attain,
Why do I suffer, Oh Lord, if I have done nothing wrong,
What penance am I paying, to want something that I
    will never get?

BRUNO

In ogni oggetto c'è un'idea
in ogni idea c'è un'ombra
quell'ombra è lo specchio
dell'infinito e delle profondità
dentre delle quali troviamo verità,
la verità più grande
che si possa scoprire: Il segretto dell'universo.

WALID

Sefa, I am fighting for our freedom, and these people
want to take it away from you. I am here to protect you.
They want a future without us, but we have a right to
a future too.

They see the Day indeed as a far-off event, but we see
it quite near. The Day that the sky will be like molten
brass, and the mountains will be like wool, and no
friend will ask after a friend, though they will be put
in sight of each other, the sinner's desire will be that

he could redeem himself from the penalty of that day by sacrificing his children, his wife and his brother, his kindred who sheltered him, and all, all that is on earth, so it could deliver him: by no means! For it would be the Fire of Hell! Plucking out (his being) right to the skull! Inviting all such as turn their backs and turn away their faces.

RINALDO
¡Dios mío, soy yo! ¡Yo en el sepulcro!
Y mi amada Dorotea con Torrijos.
No, no será eso lo que mi futuro acarrea,
¡Morir sin hijos, sin amor, sin luto,
Enfrentar la nada!
No permitiré yo a los cielos tal tarea,
Y Torrijos no me sobrevivirá ileso,
Pues probará antes mi espada.

SEFA
And then I saw the wounded man, hiding under the bridge. He couldn't move. The men from my neighborhood came in the morning looking for him, but I knew if I told them where he was, they would kill him.

IL GIUDICE
Rifiuti la tua affermazione che l'universo è infinito, che consiste in un'immensa regione eterea; che il sole, la luna e innumerabili altri corpi celesti si trovano in questa regione; che non si deve credere che ci sia firmamento?

BRUNO
Magari mi giudicate, pensando d'essere dotati d'un potere divino; ma quel potere divino risiede in ogni oggetto ed ogni essere umano. Come potrei ritrattare quello che

so d'essere la verità, quello che è la legge basilare del universo? Giudici, siate cauti nel vostro verdetto, perchè verrate giudicati allo stesso modo anche voi!

EMILY
Rick, don't leave, please. I need you. I need your strength with me.

RICK
Miss Emily . . . there is nothing I can do for you.

EMILY
You resent me, don't you? You do, don't you?

RICK
I never existed for you. I was invisible. You only see me now because you are weak, because you are confused. But it doesn't matter, because I can't do anything about it. I wish I could. I really do.

EMILY
I just want you to be with me. Please don't treat me the way I have treated you . . .

RICK
The time has come, Miss Emily, it is time for you to leave. We have to leave.

SEFA
Walid says that tomorrow we have to leave Jahannam, that it is not safe for us to be here. But we cannot leave. My mother says that what good is it for them to leave their only home, what is the point.

WALID
But those who reject Faith and treat our signs as false-
hoods, they will be companions of the fire, to dwell
therein for aye: and evil is that goal. No kind of calamity
can occur, except by the leave of Allah: and if anyone
believes in Allah, Allah guides his heart: for Allah knows
all things. So obey Allah, and obey His Apostle: but if
ye turn back, the duty of Our Apostle is but to proclaim
the Message clearly and openly.

RINALDO
Sólo resta esperar. Esta noche, Torrijos, será tu última,
Y después de penetrar mi espada tu traicionero cuerpo,
Ínfima memoria serás, y al callar tus ojos fijos
Los míos poseerán a Dorotea, sólo para a ella amar.

EL COMENDADOR
Entro sigiloso, pues sorprender quiero a Torrijos
Con las nuevas de mi decisión. Nuevo hijo tendré
Al casar mi hija con él y adquirir noble posición.

RINALDO
¡Alerta! Pasos oigo. De atacar es hora.
(*Rinaldo hiere al Comendador*)
¡Muere, desgraciado!

EL COMENDADOR
¡Por Cristo! Rinaldo, me has herido.

RINALDO
¡Comendador! ¿Como ha sido?
¡Oh, que me lleve el infierno!
(*Entran Torrijios y Dorotea*)

TORRIJOS

¿Qué bulla oigo en mi casa?
¿Pero qué veo? Rinaldo ha herido a tu padre!
A ti te daré caza, desgraciado, por mi madre!
(*Torrijos hiere a Rinaldo*)

DOROTEA

¡Deteneos Torrijos! Virgen Santa, ¡qué herida!
¿Qué ha pasado ante mis ojos?
El amor mío cae sangrando y con él mi vida.

EMILY

This place is my life, and I am part of it,
We shall never be apart. If it falls, may I fall with it.
If I were to leave with the wound, it will never heal.
I cannot conceive any other life, or any other place.

RICK

This is crazy, you cannot let yourself perish.

EMILY

It is too late to be reborn. I have played my cards, and
    I have lost.

LO SPIRITO

Sei trasgressore delle regole. Hai cercato di svelare verità
nascoste. Per quello, dovrai soffrire le conseguenze. Sei
dotato di una percezione speciale, la chiave alla comprensione del nostro mondo. Ti ho dato uno scorcio di
Paradiso, ma hai sperperato questa conoscenza. Dici di
sapere la verità, ma gli altri non ti ascolteranno, nem-
meno capiranno— sarà come se tu stessi parlando un'altra
lingua. La conoscenza conduce alla solitudine.

BRUNO

Mi avete insegnato che tutti noi, come l'universo, siamo una molteplicità di creature, una molteplicità di voci, governate dai quattro venti cardinali. Ognuna delle nostre voci fornisce una chiave alla comprensione. Datemi quella comprensione, fatemi vedere e capire cose oltre a me stesso e al mio corpo umile, oltre ai miei dubbi e le mie paure; fatemi fissare lo sguardo oltre alle rive dell'umanità che contengo dentro di me; fatemi vedere la luce dalle profondità del buio, la luce divina che emerge dalle ombre, la luce divina che emerge dalle ombre.

WALID

Your riches and your children may be but a trial: but the presence of Allah is the highest reward. So fear Allah as much as ye can; listen and obey and spend in charity for the benefit of your own soul and those saved from the covetousness of their own souls—they are the ones that will achieve prosperity.

If ye give to Allah a bountiful loan, He will double it to your credit, and He will grant you forgiveness: for Allah is most forbearing . . .

BRUNO

Ho lottato, ed è stato duro. Pensavo di poter vincere . . . ma la natura e la fortuna hanno posto fine alla mia impresa. È già qualcosa, il mero fatto che ho cominciato la lotta, perchè vedo che la vittoria depende del tutto dal destino. Dentro di me c'era quello che è possibile e quello che nessuno mi può negare: tutto quello che un vincitore può dare di sè; che non ho temuto la minaccia della morte, che sono stato sempre duro, e non mi sono sottomesso a nessuno della mia razza; che avrei preferito una morte coraggiosa ad una vita impaurita ... spacco il cielo e volo al infinito. Quello che gli altri vedono da lontano, lascio dietro di me.

EMILY
I will finally be able to fly and get away from the winter.

RINALDO
Dorotea, muero feliz de saberme amado.

SEFA
I don't like to think there is a better place than this.

BRUNO
Chi non si eleva ai pari di Dio non lo può mai capire, perchè il simile non è intelleggibile tranne al simile. Vola alle altezze d'una grandezza oltre misura, liberati dai confini del corpo, trascendi la temporalità, diventa l'Eternità sè stessa; solo allora potrai conoscere Dio. Credi che niente sia impossibile per te; credi d'essere immortale e capace d'una comprensione universale, di tutte le arti e le scienze, e della natura d'ogni essere umano. Vada oltre all'altezza più alta e la profondità più profonda. Senti tutte le sensazioni della Creazione— del fuoco e dell'acqua, del secco e del umido— immaginando che la tua anima si estendi dovunque, sulla terra e nel mare, al cielo; che tu non sia ancora nato, che sia ancora nel utero materno, che sia adolescente, vecchio, morto, oltre alla morte.

Se accogli i tuoi pensieri, e tutte le cose ad una volta: le epoche, i luoghi, le sostanze, le quantità— allora capirai che cos'è Dio.

O sfere luminose,
O guardiani dei segreti e le verità della natura,
Siete la scala dove la natura scende alla produzione di
    tutte le cose
E dove l'intelletto sale alla conoscenza di tali cose,
L'uno e l'altro tornano all'untità.

EMILY
In life, we build castles that slowly wash away, in death,
we wash away and a castle that is built upon us . . .

RINALDO
Parte ya mi alma, termina mi desvelo.
Infeliz vida he vivido, mas muero satisfecho.
Se me ha dado la verdad de la tierra y del cielo.
Mi amor, nunca consumado, fue un hecho,
Y sé que una vez habiendo partido
Mi memoria no será perdida,
Sino que persistirá, como la hiedra
Que dará nombre a cada sombra, y a cada piedra
Vosotros en mí y yo en vosotros,
Un hechizo de Tepoztlán me hizo errar
Pero fue en mis errores que hallé la medida,
Y serán ellos que muestren la verdad
Para los otros que vengan a la tierra
Y sepan leer entre las líneas de la vida.

Author's Profile

Pablo Helguera was born in 1971 in the neighbor-hood of Tacuyaba, Mexico City. According to his words, "from as far as I can remember, I have held an almost existential obsession with three things: nostalgia, fic-tion, and the meaning of art." His family remembers that, upon hearing a musical piece at four years old, Helguera said: "I like this music very much; it reminds me of my childhood." As a member of a family that has had classical music as a profession for three generations, he took piano and voice lessons from an early age but later, and inexplicably, turned to the visual arts. In one of his first exhibitions, *Babel* (1993), which took place at the Art Institute of Chicago, Helguera completely re-staged a casual photograph of his father and a busi-nessman from Chicago taken in Xochimilco in 1943. In 1994, having discovered performance art as his strange calling, he founded the failed *Circorama de la Nostalgia Operistica* (Circorama of Operistic Nostalgia), a project that consisted of facilitating the experience of strange, memorable, and temporary moments to the audience. The exhibit *Estacionamientos* (Parking Zones; 1998), pre-sented at the Tallería Gallery in Mexico's Colonia Roma neighborhood, was a "multi-individual" or "uni-collective" exhibition that presented fourteen fictional artists with different styles, ages, origins and appearances. *Parallel Lives* (2003), presented at New York's Museum of Modern Art and at the Julia Friedman Gallery, consisted of the reconstruction of the lives of five idealistic and eccentric characters, all of whom were misunderstood during their time: Friederick Froebel (the inventor of Kindergarten),

Florence Foster Jenkins (the worst soprano in history), Giulio Camillo (the creator of a theater of memory), Ward Jackson (The Guggenheim Museum's archivist), and the Shakers (a nearly extinct religious group in the United States). The exhibition, with an acoustic guide narrated by Fred Wilson, contained various objects that simultaneously illustrated the five biographies.

Most recently, Helguera developed the projects *Conservatorio de lenguas muertas* (Conservatory of Dead Languages; 2004), a compilation of phonographic recordings of dying languages. He also created *The School of Panamerican Unrest*, a portable collapsible schoolhouse that he transported on a van down the Pan-American Highway, from Alaska to Tierra del Fuego, making various stops and performances in between. His work is part of the collection of New York's Museo del Barrio and many other institutions and museums. In 2005, he presented the performance *The Foreign Legion*, an opera that consists of four round table discussions that alternate with one another. He is the author of the books *Endingness* (2005), an essay on the art of memory; the *Manual of Contemporary Art Style* (Spanish version: 2005; English version: 2007), an etiquette manual for the art world; and *The Boy Inside the Letter* (2008). He has been the recipient of the Guggenheim Fellowship and a Creative Capital grant. He is currently the director of Adult and Academic Programs at New York's Museum of Modern Art. He lives in Brooklyn, New York.

www.ingramcontent.com/pod-product-compliance
Lightning Source LLC
Chambersburg PA
CBHW030528260626
47157CB00005B/1923